The Knife

by

R S Cannan

To Robin + Dave
Best Friend
(d (Dick) Cannan

AuthorHouse™
1663 Liberty Drive
Bloomington, IN 47403
www.authorhouse.com
Phone: 1-800-839-8640

First published by AuthorHouse 08/29/2011

ISBN: 978-1-4634-4564-5 (sc)

Library of Congress Control Number: 2011914196

Printed in the United States of America

authorHOUSE®

Dedication:

This story was written for Brennan and Shaun. A small legacy from me to you I hope you enjoy it.

Love,
Poppa

THE KNIFE

INTRODUCTION

This is a tale of discovery, history and what I went through in the early fall of 1996. Some will believe it as true and factual and some will say that it is the hallucinations of a man that has spent too long in the wilderness alone. I can only report what is, to the best of my knowledge the facts of this expedition and leave you to determine what is truth and what are the failings of the mind.

THE HUNT

This starts out in the early spring of 1996. I applied to the Montana department of conservation for a fall bow hunting tag for elk   I received my tag in the late summer and was as excited as a person could be. I had been applying for several years with no luck. This was going to be my time. I applied for two weeks vacation from work and got it. I left for Montana the first week of September, with all of the anticipation of a teenager going on his first date. My tag was good for the wildlife management unit (WMU) just north of Yellowstone National Park, covering over a thousand square miles of wilderness and mountains. I arrived in Yellowstone a few days later and begin my trek just outside the town of Corwin Springs. The weather was beautiful early fall with warm sunshine and cool evenings; I hiked for several days up hills, through the lush meadows of the high country. I spotted elk periodically all at long distances. Sleeping out under the stars was magnificent with no lights to dim the brightness of the sky I fell asleep in wonderment of the heavens.   I have always had an affinity for the constellations. My father taught me to find them and follow them through the different seasons.   I have always had an attraction to the North Star. I can't explain it but I just believe it's been my star all along. I used it several times for navigational purposes, once when I was in the service and on night maneuvers in the desert where our "leader" got us lost for almost a day and once when flying back from a weekend rendezvous of black powder shooting and debauchery. That is another tale left for later writings.

I picked out the big dipper, small dipper, Cassiopeia and to the south Orion the archer. Since I was on a bow-hunting trip I thought this was a good omen. I moved north and slightly west following my topographic maps and compass. On the fourth day out I spotted a small herd, about fifteen animals with a large bull tailing behind. This I decided was the one I was going to take, so I moved in for the stalk. Heart pounding and mouth dry, I knew this was going to be it. I called and called to get his attention, but he wouldn't leave the cows behind to investigate. The next two days, I couldn't get close to get the shot. It almost seemed he knew he was being pursued, but he didn't panic and run, just a constant slow walk and moving the herd higher and higher into the mountains. This went on for two days.   The mountains were high in this area and the temperature was starting to drop at night. I made camp and stopped for the night trying to figure out what to do next. I think I have gone too far the mountains didn't match the topo maps. I woke up to a cold rain and mist. I was tired and thought this might be a good time to rest and regroup.   It rained all day and the following

morning dawn broke with low clouds and mist so heavy you couldn't see the mountaintops only half a mile visibility. I thought I was glad not to be flying in this country with this weather. I broke camp and went looking for the herd. Nowhere to be seen - no tracks, no droppings. They were like ghosts disappearing in the mist. This is just great I thought to myself. Out here in the wilderness and so intent for the last several days that I lost track of where I was. The sun finally broke out and I felt better, I'll find them. I pulled out the topo's and sat down to figure this mess out. I finally determined where I was "approximately". To my chagrin I was near the tree line why would that bull lead the herd and me way up here where the forage was sparse with the wind and cold. It didn't make sense. I spent the next couple of days looking and scouting around to try and find the herd or some other elk. Absolutely nothing, the valleys were filled in with rain and probably snow, but I was above them in the sunshine. This lasted two days, now I was getting nowhere, no elk, and no wildlife to speak of just wide-open spaces. I noticed some weather moving in so I thought it would be wise to make camp and decide what my next move was going to be. My food supplies were running low so I decided that the next morning I'd move lower and try to find my way out.

The next day was miserable the temperatures were dropping and as I looked out of my tent everything was white. This was really a problem now. I decided to break camp and move I scoped ahead with my binoculars and saw a large out cropping of stone, so I moved toward it hoping to be able to get out of the wind and cold. I walked along the tree line and it soon became obvious I was in a box canyon. I was just moving around a big bowl. The wind was howling around 20-30 miles per hour and the temperatures would be going down. I needed to find shelter soon. I walked to the outcropping, but found it was little help. I'm tired, cold, wet and really getting hungry. I sat down trying to fight off the panic that had been building inside of me for two days. I smelled a strange odor, almost acidy but definitely the smell of rotten eggs. Where could this be coming from, I moved around a small ledge and I felt warm air on my face? This is impossible I must be dreaming. I took off my gloves and felt with my hand a warm drifting air. I pushed back some scrub bushes and small evergreens to see the wide mouth of a cave.

THE CAVE

I couldn't believe my eyes. My first instinct was to go in, but then reason took over. A cave this high up might contain more than just me. It was close to denning up time for bears and mountain lions. That is the last thing I wanted to tangle with, so I sat down at the mouth just to feel the warm air. If there is anything I hate worse is to be cold and hungry. Time was running out, I dug through my pack and found my flashlight. I thought well what the hell, I might just as well get eaten by a bear than to stay outside and freeze to death. I picked up several rocks and tossed them in one at a time to see if there was a response. Nothing just dead silence. I nocked up an arrow and put on my headlamp. I entered slowly and quietly. The cave was deep and didn't smell too good, now I know I stumbled into a bear den or something just as evil. When I was in about ten feet in, it was warm, almost enough to take off my parka. What a strange place. I went back out and retrieved my pack and placed it near the entrance. I got out a coil of parachute cord that I brought along to help secure my tent in high winds. I tied it to a small bulge of rock and began to unwind it as I walked along. I decided that I was only going in as far as the line would go. The further I went in the warmer it got and the smell got worse. This was definitely sulfur I shouldn't have been too surprised, because we were outside of Yellowstone where the hot springs and boiling mud and super springs were abundant. It was unnerving though that it should occur this high up. I noticed that there were several openings both to the left and right of me, I peaked in and the one to the right looked like it went on forever, even the bright light of the head lamp could only penetrate a couple of hundred feet. It was really warm all the way through. , I took off my parka and sweater, so I wouldn't sweat too much. Soon I was out of rope, this was truly a big cave I had no trouble standing up, I turned and started to work my way back out being careful to wind up the rope as I went. Now I was moving slowly looking around and noticing several small rooms to my right. Then I froze I heard something in front of me I could just barely make out the light at the entrance of the cave. I couldn't see anything but just felt like I wasn't alone. I turned off the headlamp and moved ever so slowly toward the entrance. I could hear my heart pounding and thought that it would give me away. Then a movement, then some more sounds almost breathing. I could recognize four legs and dark fur. It couldn't be I was alone, then more movement. It was in the cave entrance big, but not enough to fill the entrance. I tried to make some noise, but my mouth was so dry I could barely get anything out. It stopped, I yelled hey, the bear stopped and growled I moved to my right I knew he couldn't see me just coning in from the bright outside. I yelled again and this time he growled louder and made a move. I quickly moved to my left and drew the bow back. He stood up on his back legs and growled again. I had the perfect sight picture and let the arrow go. The wasp tipped arrow flew straight and true, striking him square in the chest just left of center. He let out a tremendous roar that filled the cave. I quickly nocked another arrow and got ready for the charge. He didn't move much; just dropped to all fours, turned to go, and rolled over. He let out a final feeble roar and was dead. I moved cautiously toward him picking up my rope as I moved. I just stopped and poked him with the arrow point and no movement. He was dead for sure. I think I started breathing again, because I felt short of breath and stood there looking at him. I've been scared before, but this one has to be up there with the best of them.

I walked around trying to gather my thoughts and said now what? I went back to the bear looked around the cave and noticed a small "room just to my right and I stepped in, again a putrid smell over took me, but I noticed nothing out of the ordinary. This place must have been used for years, as a winter haven for bears and other critters   I looked closely at the bear and found he wasn't as big as I first thought, maybe 150 to 175 pounds, a nice year and half boar. I dragged him outside to get a close look in the light. The arrow went through his heart and almost came out the back. At least I won't starve. The first two rules of survival in the wilderness have been met. One- shelter from the wind and elements with a source of heat. Two –food, and three- water. It was snowing pretty well now so I went to work butchering and skinning the bear.

It was almost dark when I finished. I laid the hide out staking it down just outside the cave. I cut the meat up into pieces that I could cook and eat in small amounts so the rest could be frozen. Talk about cold the temperatures it really fell off so I retreated to the warmth of the cave with some meat for dinner. I decided to spend the night right at the mouth of the cave in case I had any nighttime visitors. It was a fitful sleep, but the night went fast and soon it was early morning. The outside landscape was frosty with hazy sunshine, but the temps had to be down into the low twenties or below. I decided it was too cold to venture outside, so I set about exploring my new shelter. I repeated my process with the rope and moving back towards the darkness. I went in a far as I could and started to explore the nooks and crannies of the cave. Most were small and went nowhere and some were large enough for an animal to den-up.

Fortunately I was the only one in the back part of the cave. As I neared the entrance again   I spotted a room to my right. As I went in I found it to be larger than most, the smell was pretty pungent so I figured it was the main area that the intruder bear was heading for. I noticed near the wall a mound, and bent down to look. My god it was a skull, human to be exact. Pretty old since it was covered with dirt. I started to brush away the dirt and found more bones. It was pretty intact for a skeleton. I was not the first person to seek shelter up here. I picked up a leg bone and held it next to mine, it was smaller by a couple of inches, so I figured he was probably about 5'4" tall, maybe a little shorter. As I was moving around I found to my amazement another skull this one was different, I thought maybe an animal or something. I brushed more dirt away and found the rest of the second mans' skeleton. This one looked different and the few leg bones I found were longer. This guy had to be well over 6'. I took both skulls to the front of the cave so I could see them better. I needed to conserve my batteries in my headlamp more.

The first skull I found looked relatively normal except most of the teeth were missing

And the ones that were left weren't in very good shape. The second skull was different. The cranium shape was really different. It was elongated and larger overall. I've seen programs about aboriginal people that bound their kid's heads when they were young so they would get a very elongated heed. I suspect that's what happened to this poor fellow. But his height was also strange. His teeth were almost perfect and they were all there. He must have had a good dentist I thought. I went back into the cave room and put the skulls back. When I get out of this mess I'm going to have to report the bodies I found.

DISCOVERY

I went about trying to cover the bodies up and brushed the dirt back on them that was near by. As I was moving the dirt I brushed against something hard and metal, damn near cut my hand open on a metal box. It was probably 9 inches by 13 inches by 6 inches, I brushed away the dirt and picked it up. I took it to the cave entrance and looked at it. It was all metal, probably copper since it had a dark patina on it most of the way around. There was a latch and hinges that looked to be made of brass. I opened it up and found an old leather book and in the bottom a knife. Since I've made a couple of knives in my life I looked at it real close. The blade was steel rusted with some pitting; the handle was an antler with one tine. The blade was attached to the handle with leather like strapping in the fashion of an old arrowhead like the Indians used to do. The blade was about 3 inches or so with a modified drop point. Kind of strange for this area and with the handle so small, it would have fit a kid's hand.

I carefully opened the book and found it was written by hand in Spanish. Now my Spanish isn't very good so I started to read it slowly and carefully. I'll translate it the best I can, keeping in mind that I probably will miss a lot of words and meanings.

THE JOURNAL

It read, "This is the diary of Father Diego Sanchez dated 1535. It details the journey of myself and a group of explorers, lead by Captain Fernando Mendoza of Castillo, Spain.

We were part of the larger exploration group of Caba de Vaca directed by the king of Spain to explore the new world south and west of the territory now recognized as new Spain. We sailed abound New Spain and had a very rough voyage, I was sick most of the time at sea. We landed on a set of barrier reefs. I was in the first boat and wanted nothing more than to get off of this little boat. As soon as we landed I jumped out onto the dry land and began to wretch my guts out. Don de Vaca jumped out and watched me hurl. He laughed and said padre you're the first one here and I looked up and said I'm sorry your Excellency that was your honor. He laughed and said well I guess we'll have to call this Padre Island after you Padre Dio We traveled inland and found good land and plenty of fresh water 10 days hike inward. We established our main camp and set to work on a palisade structure that would be our home. We left to head north with a large expedition group of around several hundred people, horses and carts. We found a large river that flowed from North to South and decided to follow it as far as it would go. Our primary mission was to explore the land and find gold if possible, but mainly to find what riches the King of Spain had on his new land. I was on this mission with several other priests to minister to our people and to try to convert as many savages as possible. Language was a big problem for us since none of us spoke the native language and they had never seen white people before, some were scared of us and others were friendly. I set about teaching a few of the savages our language so we could communicate better. After several months Don de Vaca decided to branch out so we could explore more territory. I was tasked with joining Captain Mendoza's group. We were to head north and west, since one of our savage guides had told of a large set of mountains way to the west. We were a group of twenty or so men at arms, several horse packers and a couple of guides. The weather was generally warm and along the banks of the rivers lush with grass for the horses. The men were mostly soldiers that Capt Mendoza knew from the wars with England and France. They were not a Christian lot and my work with them was hard as most of them were non -believers since they got to the new world. We had several run- ins' with local natives, but the matchlock rifles we bore scared them away pretty quickly. I was to find out later that the savages were very scared of the horses, since they had not seen them either. We did have some trouble at night though with the thieves. After a month away from the main party we had a serious battle with the savages, with many of them killed and wounded. Several of our men died, and a couple were wounded by arrows. We stopped a couple of days to rest. The Captain had a couple natives that were wounded brought before him and our native guides talked with them. Once Captain Mendoza had the information he wanted from the captives he had them killed straight a way. He said he could not keep captives and feed them since they would only slow us down. He was a brutal man I think that's why some of the men called him Bastard Mendoza. I said that's not the reason he was called bastard, but because he is the bastard son of Don de Salvo of Castillo. That's why he is a soldier; he will never inherit his father's wealth. That's the way it is in Spain in the 1530s. . We kept on moving northward and we've begun to see mountains in the distance, not the small ones, but big as in the East of Spain between us and the heathen French. There was snow on the tops and the men were beginning to complain that we would never get back to the rendezvous point with de Vaca in time for Christmas.

One day one of our guides came back to tell us that a large band of natives were ahead of us, gathering at the bend of the river we were following and about an hours walk ahead of us. Captain Mendoza ordered out all of the matchlocks we had with extra powder and ball to be given to each man. I said I was a man of God and would not carry any firearms. He looked at me and said then you will die like a coward and a dog. We moved forward to meet the savages and as we came over a small hill they were there in front of us. Since we were outnumbered he said let them come to us and we will slaughter them as they come up the hill. One of the guides came up and asked to go meet with them. He said he would tell them of our great magic in the thunder sticks we carry. Captain Mendoza said okay go out to them, but you must come back or we will kill you.

Soon the guide came back and told us that they didn't believe the story of the thunder sticks and that there greatest shaman will test our magic against his. A lone native came into the open and walked about half way up to us. Captain Mendoza grabbed one of the matchlock rifles from his man at arms and galloped up to the shaman and shot him in the head from about 10 meters away. When the smoke cleared Captain Mendoza sitting on his large black horse with the sun shinning on his polished breastplate, looked down on the dead man. He got off his horse and proceeded to cut the man's head off and rode away with it hanging from his saddle. The natives retreated as fast as they could run.

Our native guides shook with fear when he came back; they told me that it was not their custom to do that to an enemy, because the man would not be allowed into the afterlife if he was not whole. They begged me to talk to the captain to allow them to return the head to the man's body so he can be buried as there custom dictated. I approached the captain and explained what they wanted to do. He said no that this would teach them that this is what will happen to them if they try to attack us again. He told his men at arms to burn the head in the campfire. I told them that I tried, but that he said no. I told them that I would pray to my God to allow this man to enter heaven. They turned and walked away. We stayed here that night. We moved on the next day and for several days after that we did not see any natives, but I felt they were watching us all along.

We continued to move north and we came upon a great river flowing high with great waves and rocks. We moved slowly trying to find a way across and soon our guides came up and said they found a shallow section to cross with a great meadow on the other side so our horses to eat the lush grass. We made our way across and found a good camping area to rest for a day or two since we have been on the move for several weeks without a meaningful rest stop. Our guides came up and said there was a large group of tonkas heading this way. They went on to describe they were great shaggy beasts that sometimes covered the whole plain and that they were good to eat, but hard to kill. Our men at arms said they would like to try to get some good meat that they were tired of beans and rice. Captain Mendoza said okay, but don't take any chances and kill only enough to eat in one day. We couldn't carry any more stuff and with the warm weather the meat will go bad fast since we didn't have enough salt to preserve it.

The men soon returned with a huge beast that would have fed the whole expedition. We soon had a raging fire going and. started to cook a large portion, enough to feed the whole camp. The guides stated that they would show me how to preserve the rest of the meat so that it wouldn't spoil and that we could eat it for days. I said okay lets try it and if the men get sick then we will cook and eat you. When the fire died down and the men had eaten, they built a stick and branch cover over the fire and hung the meat in the sticks inside. They kept the small fire going all night and into the next day. Soon the meat was done and they pulled it out. It was dry and cool and not too tough. I have a hard time eating meat and stuff that's hard, because most of my teeth are gone, the ravages of old age. We moved on the next day and we kept moving north along the river. The guides came up and said they are seeing signs of more natives, but a different group than what we have seen before. I told the captain about their discoveries and he asked why they didn't tell him directly. I said that after he killed that holy man that they were very afraid of him and, would prefer to talk to me since I said I wouldn't cut their heads off. He laughed out loud and said fine father you be the one to translate. Then we soon came upon a large stick in the ground with feathers and horns and a shield attached to it. The guides said this was a marker of these new people and that we should not cross it.

We found a well-worn path that headed north; I haven't seen a path like this before except where the tonkas had gone. We made camp that night in a clearing. We had some more meat and the guides showed me that if you boil the meat in water and add some rice that it made a great meal. I decided that I would have food as long as the meat held out.

The morning broke misty with low clouds we were getting ready to break camp when a guide came up and said we were being watched and that something was going to happen. I approached Captain Mendoza and reported what the guide said. He said Padre Dio we have been watched for the last several days and he was ready for what ever happened. Soon a native appeared outside of camp and Captain Mendoza yelled for me to bring the guides. We met the stranger and through the guides we learned that the chief and shaman wanted to talk. We said we would meet them in the clearing outside of the camp and that only a few people would be welcome to talk. I accompanied Mendoza with the guides to the clearing. We sat on blankets and Mendoza brought a barrel to sit on. He wanted to be higher in stature than the rest of the group. The natives approached with hands in front of them and palms up. I suppose this was meant to show they carried no weapons. We began by making small talk and getting the greetings out of the way. They stated, by coming we were violating their land, and they wanted to know why we were there. We told them we were travelers and that we just wanted to move through their land on our journey northward. They said they had heard about our encounter with the other people several days ago and that we slaughtered their shaman. Captain Mendoza stated that we were attacked and that he would do the same to them if they attacked us. He went on to say that he can go anywhere he wanted and didn't need anybody's permission to traverse these lands. He also stated the land belongs to the king of Spain and they were the violators. The chief said they were the Shoshone people they and their ancestors have been here since the earth began and had never have heard of the king of Spain.

I saw this was getting heated and to avoid a fight I proposed that we should share some of our food with them and try to calm things; Captain Mendoza ordered food and wine to be brought out. We ate and drank some wine, which our guests had never had before, but seemed to like it. The conversation turned to the matchlock rifles we had and they had never seen or heard of them before. Captain Mendoza said he would demonstrate how effective they were. He fired a round at a small tree about 60 meters away. When the smoke had cleared they inspected the tree and saw that it was broken in half and lying on the ground. They were amazed and talked rapidly among themselves. I asked the guide what they were saying. He said that he couldn't get all of it, but generally thought Captain Mendoza was a God or a demon and that, they needed to be careful not to anger him. I told Mendoza what was going on and he just smiled and took another swig of wine.

The shaman approached and said that they would allow us to pass through their land as long as we don't come back. He asked us what spirit guide we were using. I said that we didn't have spirit guides, only our compass and the men with us. He stated that all men have spirit guides and we just don't see them. I asked what a spirit guide is. He said they generally travel with men and they can be an animal or a spirit that moves through the forest. All you have to do is recognize them. I exclaimed we didn't believe in such things, only that God protects us and shows us the true path to salvation.

He said they have many gods that do the same thing, the wind, fire, and of course mother earth that gives them everything. I think something was lost in translation, because he didn't seem to understand only one God.

They wanted to know where we were heading and Mendoza said north and pointed out the direction. The chief claimed that nothing more was north except what we see here so why don't we just go back. Mendoza said that there is a great salt sea north and west of us from here. They said they had never seen anything like that. The chief stated that beyond their territory is just a great river with yellow rocks and an area that boils and smells bad, so it must be bad. He stated that the man-beasts live there and anybody that travels there never comes back. He said even the Crow clan doesn't go in there.

Captain Mendoza's ears perked up when he heard about the yellow rocks in the river. He asked how many and how big they were. The chief said they were all sizes with a lot of them bigger than a man could carry. Captain Mendoza jumped up and clapped his hands and said we leave at dawn. The chief said they would provide a guide through their land but he would only go as far as the river with yellow rocks and no further, because he didn't want to anger the spirits that guard this bad land. He said it would take us about a week to get there and that we should never come back. Captain Mendoza said we would come back through here on our way out. The shaman said, "no you won't because no one comes out alive".

When the men heard that we were heading for a river of golden rocks there was joyous cheering all around. Now there would be no talk of going back and returning to the rendezvous point. We left early the next morning with the Shoshone guide leading us. I didn't trust this man, I thought he would lead us into a trap, obviously Captain Mendoza thought the same thing, because he kept his rifle near by all the time We kept on the move for several days, until everyone was so tired they couldn't keep up. We decided to rest a day then push on. Everyone was on high alert, but nobody followed or came near us.

After about five days the Shoshone guide told us that we had come as far as he was allowed to go and that the river below us was the river of yellow rocks. We rushed down to find the gold. We moved up stream a little and found the yellow rocks were really rocks covered in sulfur. The smell was all around us. The disappointment was obvious, the men spent the whole day turning over rocks and splitting them to no avail. There was no gold just this beautiful river flowing south. We moved up and further north until we could hear this roaring noise and saw the boiling pools of mud, water in blue pools that if touched would boil you alive. The disappointment was terrible no gold no salt sea. The men were getting angry now all this time and trouble traveling in this wilderness was for naught. Captain Mendoza was as distraught as anyone I've ever seen. No orders were given, no direction of what we're going to do next, nothing. We made camp that night and ate the last of our meat. Finally Captain Mendoza said we would start our return in the morning.

I woke early before dawn and went to the river to drink and cool my feet, it was hot and the day promised to be hotter than most. The mist was all around us so thick you couldn't see across the river. I felt I was being watched so I casually made my way back to camp. That's when I noticed all of the native guides were gone. They must have slipped out during the night. I went to wake Captain Mendoza. I told him something was wrong, that the guides had disappeared and that a strange mist had fallen over the camp. He rousted the men and told them to be quiet and to get prepared for battle.

The rifles were loaded and the matches lit. Then came a loud shriek or howl that was totally unheard of before. Arrows were flying out from the mist and the first volley took down several men. They were dead before they hit the ground. Captain Mendoza ordered the men to fire at will into the mist even though they couldn't see anything. The rifles bellowed and the smoke joined with the mist to make a cloud no one could see through. There was yelling and howling like I had never heard before another volley roared, this time they must have struck home because there were anguished cries of pain. I saw an arrow hit Captain Mendoza Square in the chest, but it glanced off and shattered.

We could barely see anything, but it looked like large shadows moving around just out of clear vision range. Soon the arrows stopped flying and everything was quiet. Captain Mendoza ordered everyone to regroup on him. It was obvious that we had taken a terrible beating. Only ten men survived and of those three had been wounded by arrows.

Captain Mendoza ordered everyone to gather as much of his or her belongings as they could carry and to move slowly and cautiously through the valley and up on the hill that overlooked the river. The horses were packed up quickly with guns, powder and shot and what little food we had left. We moved out within an hour with a lot of the men standing guard as we retreated up the hill. The men that were dead were left as they fell. I told the captain that we should at least bury them and give them a Christian service. He said if I wanted to do that, then I could stay behind. I said prayers over them and left them there. The Captain said they were good men but they weren't good Christians. We moved higher thinking we would be attacked at any time. The sun was hot and burned off the mist around noon. We could see the bodies of our downed men were gone by this time. Nobody could tell what had attacked us, only vague images. The men were superstitious and thought they were demons or spirits. The Captain laughed, and said that demons and spirits don't cry out when hit by musket balls, he calmed the men down and said they were just men and they bleed and die like other men. He acknowledged though that they were generally bigger than most men. He said he saw one up close, they had on some kind of animal skin he said he saw bear, another man said no it was a wolf and gray. We knew that we were likely to face another attack so Captain Mendoza had the men pile our travel goods and our carts, so we could protect ourselves from all directions. I had to admit that even though he was a bastard, he knew how to fight and keep men from panicking. Night came, but we built no fire so we could see them coming without them seeing us. Guards stood watch all night; I stayed awake and prayed with the ones that wanted to. Fighting men seem to find God very quickly when they think they are about to die. We heard sounds all night, the kind that sent shivers down your spine when you are facing the unknown. Just before dawn, like the day before the howling started again, but this time something else, a sort of clicking sound like thin pieces of wood being hit together. Then they came at us. The rifles roared and arrows started to fly. I ducked and hid behind the cart. Our men started to fall. Captain Mendoza stood up in a squat to fire his rifle and he was struck in the chest with an arrow, this time it went through his breastplate and he fell mortally wounded. The arrow shaft was sticking out of his chest. I went to him to see what I could do. It went almost all the way through. This was impossible stone headed arrows could not penetrate steel armor.

A man at arms came over and looked at the hole, he broke the arrow off and pulled the breastplate away from his chest. The Captain died right then. I looked at the breastplate and said that it was a strange hole, it was square not round. The man at arms said that he had seen a hole like that before, when he was with the captain fighting the English. It was a point the English had made to penetrate armor. They called it a bodkin point. Since the captain was dead he pulled the arrow out and sure enough it was a long square point made of steel. His eyes got big and said that these beast-men had steel, which was quite impossible since we were the first white men in this country as evidenced by what all of the savages had told us.

The men that still lived decide to take their chances and run. I prayed for the dead and dying and thought this was the end of me. The men that ran went in all directions except north and as I prayed I could hear them being cut down. I trembled in fear until the noise subsided and I grabbed my water skin and crawled away in the mist. I went north. As soon as I got further away and I couldn't see the camp I ran towards the river. I swam across with great difficulty with my water skin and my shoulder bag that carried my bible, my journal and some left over food scraps. When I got to the other side I ran towards the trees. When I got into the forest I sat down and tried to collect my thoughts.

I don't know how long I stayed there, but I moved a little and sat down and then moved a little and sat down. I was heading up hill and decided to keep on going for a while to see where I would end up. I knew downhill near the river was not the place to go since that was where the rest of the party was killed. I didn't want to think of all the men that I had traveled with were now dead. I kept going up.

I felt that I was being watched, but just passed it off as being scared. I moved ever upward. I did this for a couple of days, but quite honestly I was losing track of time. Then it happened, an arrow flew out of the woods and struck a rock next to me and flew into my leg. The pain was intense I looked down and saw it went straight through with both ends sticking out. I broke the arrow off and threw it away. I noticed it was a simple stone headed arrow. I wrapped a part of my shirt around my leg and kept moving. I thought I would try to hide from the man-beast if I could find somewhere to get into. I couldn't see him, but I heard rocks falling as he made his way toward me. I lay down in a thicket and prayed. He had stopped moving also waiting for me to make my first move. I remembered years ago that my father told me that a rabbit always gets caught when he moves and rarely gets caught when he stays perfectly still. I stayed perfectly still. Some time went by and I heard him move off. I stayed still a while longer then moved quietly as I could in another direction. I moved along a tree line until it was starting to get dark so I knew I had to hole up for awhile at night. A little further away. I sat down for a rest and then I heard a noise. I looked to my right and a small red fox jumped out of the brush and sat there looking at me. He scampered off and then sat down looked at me some more and moved some more. I thought he might know where he was so I followed him. He would never let me get close to him, but obviously he wanted me to follow him. I kept moving along for an hour or so in the dimming light, I saw a big outcropping of rock. The fox moved in that direction so I moved with him. He went by it and thought that would be a good place to hide. So I moved in that direction. About an hour later I came up to the outcropping and moved against the stone wall. I felt a warm breeze near my back and I moved a little bit more. Here was my hideout, a cave in the wall where the warm breeze came from. It was dark inside so I couldn't see much, so I went in only as far as the light would allow. I looked out and the fox was nowhere to be seen. I sat down to rest and I think I fell asleep, because when I awoke it was dark outside as well as in the cave. It was a restless night because I kept worrying about the man-beast that was following me. I hope I lost him. My leg was hurting me very much and I tried to wrap more clothing around it to stop the bleeding.

When dawn broke I was tired and cramped up from the day before's running and crawling around in the brush. I drank some water and poked my head out. It was bright sunshine and my hopes began to take off, not seeing anything I got up and walked a little bit to straighten up. Until I saw something, just a movement and then it became clear it was large and black. He got up and walked on two feet. I thought it was a bear, but it didn't move like one. When I was young, I had seen one at a fair. It was the man-beast that had followed me. He was tracking the blood trail from my leg. I knew I was trapped in the cave, what could I do? I was scared and thought this was the end, killed by a man-beast in the wilderness. I just sat down resigned to my fate, as I sat back a rock came loose from the wall. I looked around and there was a dark corner and a small ledge. I grabbed the rock and stood on the ledge and waited. The man-beast came near the entrance and looked in. My heart was pounding in my chest I thought he could hear it beating. He came in a few steps and looked around then a few more, his back was to me and I was taller than he was. I jumped off the ledge and at the same time brought the stone down as hard as I could. I missed his head, but I heard a big thump and we both went down to the ground. I rolled over and got to my feet as fast as I could to strike another blow. He was on his back; his legs and arms were shaking and twitching. This ended soon and he just laid there a low groan came out. I killed the man-beast I thought right off. I poked him with the bow that he had been carrying, but didn't move, just groaned. Now what do I do. I sat down for a couple of minutes to see if he would just die. He didn't so I thought I'd just hit him with the rock again. I poked him again and he moaned, but almost a word sound came out. I asked him if he heard and another sound came out like a word. I reached down and looked at his head; he was wearing a bear head and pelt over him. I reached up and pulled the bear head off. He was a man. I looked at him and he was like a native man, except that his skin was lighter and it had a grayish brown tint to it. His eyes were a little larger than normal. They were black, not dark brown but black as coal. His hair was black and straight like the natives we had seen. Now that I saw him he was just a man I felt sorry for him. I'm not a killer like Captain Mendoza was. I gave him a sip of my water and he gratefully accepted it. He couldn't move except for his head back and forth. I started talking to him that I was sorry for hurting him and that he shouldn't have tried to kill me with his bow. I just babbled on and the look in his eyes was sort of fearful and understanding at the same time, if that is possible.

I went on and on just talking and babbling on about what ever came into my mind. He just kept looking at me. Finally I said my name was Padre Dio and what's yours?

He came right back with Locano. I was amazed that he talked, much less understood my question. I asked if he understood me. He said a little, I asked where he learned Spanish. He said he didn't, but that new languages were easy for him, all he had to do was listen to what I was saying. I asked him if he was Sash one or Crow. He said no he was Assanti.

I had never had heard of them before. He said they are an old people that had lived here in the mountains for a long time. He said his ancestors had come here from far away. I told him I had come a long way also and that this was a new place for me. He asked where I came from, I said from across the sea to the east of here. I asked why they attacked us and why he attacked me. He said they generally attack anyone that comes into their territory and it was just their way, they didn't want any contact with other people unless they initiate it. I just kept writing in my journal. He asked what I was doing and I said I was keeping a journal. I write down the people I meet and the places I go. I asked if he could write. He looked bewildered; he didn't know how to write. I showed him what I had written and he just stared at it. He later said that they didn't write, but they tell stories about what has happened in the past and they just pass things on that way.

I asked him if he hurt any place, he said no that he couldn't feel anything from his head down and that he couldn't move his arms or legs. I said that I was sorry for hitting him and injuring him so badly. He said that it was all right, that he had tried to kill me and that I was only doing what I thought was right. He said he didn't blame me, that it was probably time for him to die any ways

My leg was killing me, I looked at the wound and it was beginning to turn red, but the blood had stopped pouring out. I took a cloth from my bag and put some herbs that I always carry with me and wrapped them up. I limped out to the front of the cave and wrapped snow around the small bag then came back inside. I placed it on my leg and the warmth melted the snow and made a wet poltice. The weather had turned bad, but the unusual warmth of the cave made it very comfortable. I had some water from my skin and offered it to Locano; he looked at me strange like and asked why I was being so good to him. I said I was a priest and that it was my job to help others. I said a priest is like a shaman in his culture. We were both tired and I fell asleep.

When I awoke it was dark so I couldn't do anything except try to sleep again. My leg was not much better by the following morning. Locano was awake, just staring at me.

I looked around to find something to eat, but nothing edible was in the cave and I didn't have anything. I asked Locano if he had anything to eat, he said there was some dried meat in his bag. I opened it and found the meat some stones and a little dried grass and wood chips in a small leather bag. He said that if I could find some dry wood outside of the cave, that we could make a fire.

I thought that I might be able to find some, so I limped out outside and found the dry twigs and a small fallen tree so I dragged them in.

I asked him how to start a fire. He laughed and said put the dry grass on the ground where it's flat and break up the twigs and strike the stones together to make a spark on the grass. After several attempts the grass caught fire. We chewed on the dried meat and talked about our homes. This went on for several days and his language skills kept increasing at an incredible rate, until he was fluent. I never got passed the first few words of his language. What an incredible mind he must have.

I asked him about his ancestors and he went on to say that: They were a very old people that had come here from a long ways away many seasons ago. He said that his grandfather was very old when he died, probably 200 years old. He said that his father was killed by some other tribe; I suspect they were Crow or Shoshone. His mother had died giving birth, as most of the women did. He said that when the ancestors came to this place, they brought no women with them, and that was the reason they came here. He said there were problems with his people they needed to have some new women to keep the Assanti tribe alive. Their numbers keep going down and soon they would be gone. He said that the women always have trouble giving birth to children why he didn't know. He said they would raid other tribes and take a few young women away. He thinks this is why the other tribes keep attacking them. He said some children die before they're born so the numbers keep getting smaller. I asked him how old he was and he said he thought about fifty seasons, but didn't really know for sure. He said he didn't have any children. I said I didn't have any either. He looked down and said every man needs to have a legacy, something to pass on to his children and grand children. I said I agree, but neither one of us will have a legacy unless we can get some help and get out of here. He said he couldn't travel and that he was going to die here. I thought he was right; my leg was getting worse and was starting to smell bad. I knew this wasn't good, I had seen other men die from this the wound turns black and green.

I kept the fire going and we had some light through the night. Locano awoke the next morning with a cough and feeling cold, and then hot, I took off his shirt so he could cool down. He was very thin almost nothing but skin and bones; He said that all his people were this way with very long legs and arms, big elongated heads and black eyes. I asked if he was born this way or if they bound his head up to make it long. He said no that was the way he was born, and he suspected that was the reason the women had trouble giving birth to his people. He said he asked his grandfather once about it and he said that where they come from that was the way everybody looked.

We got talking about the last battle and what happened. He said they had been watching us from a distance and were thinking about leaving us alone, and then they saw the large animals we had with us and wanted to take a closer look. He said they came in close and someone saw them and sounded the alarm. Soon the men were starting to point the big sticks at us and the fire came out. We attacked, then the man with the silver skin was on the big animal and moving around so fast we got scared and moved off. We lost several men. You moved up the hill and we knew we couldn't let you get by us. We talked about how to attack the men with the silver skin our arrows just bounced off of him. We finally decided the only thing we could think of and that was the sacred arrow. My friend Tallor had them. They are very sacred to us, since his grandfather and his father handed them down to him. We carry them only because they bring us good luck and we don't use them except for sacred ceremonies and show. We didn't ever want to lose them. We felt we had no choice but to use them to kill the man with the silver skin. It worked and we kept up the attack. I asked if any of my men got a way. He said no they were all killed, but that his men were killed also. He said he saw me run to the river and decided to follow to make sure I did not get away to tell other people like us they were there. I said I felt sad we're the last of our groups and that no one will know what happened. I said that is why I write in the journal, so that if it is found they will know how we lived and how we died. Locano said that it was good that I did this; I asked Locano if he would like me to write down his story so that he would be able to leave a legacy also. He thought and smiled and said that it would be a good thing to do. My people only have their stories and when the last one dies that the stories die with them.

He said that his people came from a long distance away; he asked if it was nighttime and I said yes, it's clear and starry. He asked me to take him out side. I dragged him by his fur coat to the outside of the cave. He looked up and stared at the stars for a while then said there. I looked where he was looking he said the three stars in a row It took me some time, but I found them in the southwestern sky. I said that it was the constellation Orion and that he was the archer. The three stars were his belt. Locano said that his people originally came from the third star on the right, which he called Assanti. That's why they're called the Assanti. I said that's impossible that men can't travel between the stars that even the constellations were a myth. He said his grandfather didn't lie and that it was the truth. He said they were explorers and they came here looking for ways to repopulate their world. He said they went all around but couldn't find anything or anyone to help. He said they would contact other peoples and give them a little bit of information so they would help them. I said that's how the Angelos got the arrowheads that penetrate armor. He just shrugged and said it was up to the people to decide how to use the information they gave them. He said they came to this place, because of the black rocks that were here. He said a small group decided to stay because the high ground here was good for them to breath. He said we can't stay too long down by the big waters; it was too difficult for them to breath down there. He said that his ancestors left sign posts around all the places they visited so they could always get back there. I asked what they were; he said he didn't know; that information was lost when the others left to go exploring other places. I asked how many were there, he said, thirteen that was what he was told. They were supposed to come back and pick them up later, but they never returned. Locano said he was tired now and wanted to sleep. We both drifted off, I couldn't help but think that this was impossible, that his story doesn't make sense, people no matter how different they looked couldn't travel between the stars, and it just doesn't make sense. I hurt really badly all the next day; Locano just slept most of the time. We both awoke the next day weak and hurting. I got some more water and Locano said he didn't want to drink; he was just tired and wanted to sleep. He said to get him his bag. I brought it over to him and he said dump it out. I did. In the bottom was a knife made of antler and steel. I handed it to him. He said that his grandfather gave this to him and that it was very old. He said take it, it's yours and put it with my journal.

It was his legacy to me and someday if the journal is found then it will be found and that his people will go on. He said the knife was very special to him and it possessed good luck. I said I would take care of it. He said I was a good friend and he was glad we met and we didn't kill each other. I said I was glad he didn't kill me and that I didn't kill him. He smiled and went back to sleep. I couldn't help but feel sad; we were both at our ends. I never thought it would end this way. Later that night Locano coughed and gagged a bit and died. Now I was all-alone, just me my journal and the knife. The following day I awoke with a terrible fever. I couldn't move and I could barely write. The fire was going out since I couldn't get firewood. I felt at ease; I was with my friend and I knew it was time. I think it was December 1st. I couldn't write anymore so I closed the journal. I wrapped up the journal, put the knife in the bottom of my travel box, and closed the top. It was time to sleep now.

THE WAY HOME

What an incredible tale - I can't believe it. Is this a hoax? Is this real? I will have to think on this one a while. I think I better take a rest then figure out how to get out of this mess. It was still miserable outside so I'll stay a while and let dawn break before I start out.

I woke with a start, something was different, the vibration, the whole cave was vibrating, and then the smell and it smelled terrible, sulfur. I started to get my things together, when a low rumble echoed through the cave and the vibration got more intense. I had to get out of here, something was wrong. I grabbed my pack, my bow and other clothes and ran out of the cave. My God I forgot the journal and knife. I went back in groped around in the dark and found the knife. I felt for the journal and a loud roar came out with smoke and gas. I dropped the journal and fled the cave. I was almost out cold when I got to the fresh air, coughing and spitting up. I grabbed some snow and washed my eyes out. They burnt like crazy. My face was hot and burning along with my hands. I stumbled down the ledge a ways and felt the earth trembling and shaking. The rock ledge gave away and came tumbling down obliterating the cave. I rested there in the snow until dawn, thinking about what happened and how lucky I was. At least Padre Dio and Locano were buried together for all time.

I started back down in the snow tracking very carefully in the ice and snow. I felt alone and wondered how this is going to work out. Will I be buried up here all alone?

I remembered that one of the first rules of survival was to walk down hill if possible until you find a stream, then follow the stream till you get to a river, then follow the river to civilization. I entered a thick fog bank so I thought I'd sit and wait for it to rise so I could see where I was going. I made a rough camp and waited, I took stock of my stores. Pretty thin! Just a couple of hunks of dried bear meat, and a canteen of water, but I've got plenty of snow. I think I stayed there pretty much the whole day and into the night. The following morning it was brighter but the rain was falling and I took out my compass to get a heading. The damn thing just went around in circles. I must be sitting on a pile of iron ore or something to make it act this way. Oh well! Just keep heading down hill. I was moving slowly when I saw movement. It was the same big bull elk. He turned and ambled off. I couldn't get a shot. I started to follow him as he worked his way around the tree line and down into the forest. I caught glimpses of him every couple of minutes. I saw a couple of his cows so I kept moving and stalking. Then he was gone again into the woodland. I moved slowly but surely down hill. The temperature was turning warmer as I moved through the day. Sometimes I could almost see the sun as it peeked around clouds.

I came to a small stream so I rested and filled my canteen, ate some bear meat, and thought about the cave, the knife, and the journal. Boy, I wished I could have gotten that journal. I guess I'm lucky to be alive so what's the difference. How am I going to explain what happened and what I found? I wonder if it wouldn't be best if I just said nothing at all and just let it go. I started to move again and up ahead through the pines I caught a glimpse of a shadow or something moving, it was the big bull. I moved in for the shot and he moved off. God! What a frustrating thing! This guy seems to know just when I'm getting ready to shot. He doesn't panic and run, he just moves on. He seems to be heading in my direction down hill. I kept this up all day. The stream I was following was getting bigger as we moved on; soon it was raging and turned into almost a river. I found a nice flat spot in a small meadow, so I decided to make camp for the night and get an early start in the morning, maybe I could pick up the trail of the elk. When morning broke it was bright and sunny. This made me feel better and I decided to get out of here and get back to the trailhead where I left my car. It can't be too far a way now; I've been traveling for several days now I think. Still moving down hill the stream turned into a river, I thought this must be the Yellowstone. I followed it and the walking became easier.

I saw the big elk only a couple of times today but he was still heading down and I hoped it was the direction I should be going. Wouldn't it be ironic if he was leading me out of the wilderness almost like a guide? No it couldn't be. I walked all day enjoying the sun and cool air. It was turning dark now so I should make camp, but I felt I was close. I came out into a small clearing and lo and behold there was a gravel road. Was this the road I drove in on? Do I turn left or right? I went right since it was slightly down hill. It was almost dark now and I stumbled and walked and stumbled again then I came to a paved road, I tripped on the pavement and fell down, as I was getting up I looked across the road and there he was big as ever just watching me. A blinding light hit my eyes and by the time I got adjusted a truck came to a screeching halt. The big burly driver got out and I said did you see him, he said see what? That big elk I was following. He said mister you need help there hasn't been elk in this territory since the mid seventies or eighties. Can I give you a lift, you look terrible.

He took me to Canyon Gap, where he dropped me at a clinic. When I woke up a large man with a uniform was staring down at me. He said son what's your name and where are you from? I said Dick Cannan and I'm from Rochester, New York why? He said a lot of people are worried about you, you've been reported missing for almost a month now. I said no way I've only been gone about ten days. He laughed and said it's October 13th and you've been gone a while. I called the missing persons bureau and they've notified your family. I couldn't believe what he told me, he went on to say that the rental car people notified the police when I became overdue on bringing the car back. They then notified the police in your hometown. We found your car at the trailhead and towed it back to the station. I said that's why I couldn't find it. He said mister you were twenty miles off course when Sam the logging camp driver picked you up.

I still can't believe I was gone that long, time just slipped by me up there in the high country. The next day I flew back to Rochester to a relieved family. They made me promise that I would never do that again; I said I wouldn't until the next time. I never told them what I found and time went on, until about a year ago when a friend of mine asked me what happened when I got lost in the wilderness. I said Galen I never got lost, I might have been temporarily disoriented, but never lost. After a few Old Bushmills I broke down and told him the story. He said," Man your crazy it never happened". I said oh yeah, **I've got the knife**.

EPILOGUE

The following morning Galen stopped by and said let me see the knife. I pulled it out of the safe and showed it to him. He couldn't believe his eyes. He said let me take it to work and test it to make sure its real and not a hoax. I hesitated and said okay as long, as you don't harm it or destroy it. He said no problem, the most he would do is to take a few filings from it when he sharpens it. Galen Robinso is a PHD in metallurgy at the Uof R. I told him he had to keep it secret and not tell anyone about it or where he got it. I did tell him in the end it would be good to know if I was imagining things or having hallucinations. I've dreamt many times about my adventure and wonder now if it really happened.

A few weeks later Galen came over so excited and could hardly contain himself. He started off by saying that the carbon 14 dating on the handle, blade and binding was from the late 1300's to early 1400's but not more than 1420. This would make it almost 200 years before Locano's time, which would put it right at his grandfathers early years. Galen said the handle was definitely white tail deer and the bindings were also white tail leg sineu. Although, white tails are not known to be high altitude creatures, they could have come down or traded with another lower level tribe. Galen said you haven't heard the best part.

The blade is made from high carbon steel that would-be similar to what we have today, but its carbon 14 dating is the same as the handle. That's impossible, they didn't have high carbon steel in those days, and also there are trace elements in the steel that we can't identify. I said look at your periodic table and it will be there he said he did and it doesn't exist. There's not very much, but its there. He said the other strange thing about it is the blade was cast and not forged. I said Galen mankind has been sand casting metals for over 5000 years it's not a new process. He said true enough, but this was not sand casted, sand casting leaves minute traces of sand in the metal and this has none of it. It does however have granite particles in it. Granite, you can't make a casting out of granite, it's too hard and especially in the late 1300's they didn't have the tooling to cut and smooth the casting. He said true enough, but that's what was done. There weren't even microscopic tool marks from the casting or finishing process. There was however a very small mark in the blade by the handle, it was engraved not casted in, it looks like a makers mark. I asked what it looked like he said an infinity sign, except both ends are open. That's interesting; at least I know I'm not crazy. Galen said you've got to tell people about this, we need to study it more and figure out what this is all about. I said no Galen it is what it is. He said by the way a colleague of his, Jim Whitefoot, stopped into the lab and saw me working on the knife and asked me where I got it. I said a friend. He looked at it and said it looked like a Shoshone blade shape, but different. He said he would like to study it some more and find out where it came from. I said no it was a friend and was not to be messed with, he said it might have been stolen from a sacred burial site and would need to be returned. I told him that it was a fake and that I was just proving it. I thanked Galen and put the knife back in the safe. As Galen was leaving he said, oh I almost forgot one other thing. I tried passing an electrical charge through it and guess what. I said, "I don't know, I've had enough surprises for the day". The handle is a perfect insulator from the blade, and the clear paste substance is really a form of resin emitted from trees, dated to the late 1300's. The blade not only conducts the electrical charge, but also actually intensifies it. Very strange, I've never seen anything like it I'd keep it away from any electrical circuits if I were you.

I decided that I would write this down, only for posterity's sake and nothing else.

CPSIA information can be obtained
at www.ICGtesting.com
Printed in the USA
252067LV00002B